CH

D0427137

Disney

Anna & Elsa

Anna Takes Charge

For Mary Welch —E.D.

randomhousekids.com

ISBN 978-0-7364-3480-5 (hc) — ISBN 978-0-7364-8236-3 (lib. bdg.)

Printed in the United States of America

10 9 8 7 6 5 4 3 2 1

Disney
Anna & Elsa
Anna Takes Charge

By Erica David
Illustrated by Bill Robinson,
Manuela Razzi, Francesco Legramandi,
and Gabriella Matta

Random House 🏠 New York

Chapter 1

If Anna had to pick two words to describe Arendelle, they would be "busy" and "busier." The whole village was alive with activity. Chef Florian, the owner of Florian's Famous Flangendorfers, was busy baking tasty desserts by the dozen. Nervous Norvald, the milliner, was busy making fancy hat after fancy hat. Oaken,

the owner of Wandering Oaken's Trading
Post and Sauna, was busy planning his
next big blowout sale. Anna herself had
spent all week busy with her own spring
chores. Today, she was hoping to make
time for a little adventure.

"What do you say, Elsa? Ready to
climb Mount Haraldsdottir?" Anna asked,

holding up a pair of mountain climbing boots.

Elsa sat back and sighed. She looked at Anna over the huge stack of papers on her desk. Between the spring planting projects in Arendelle and the trade deal with Tikaani, she barely had time to climb the mountain of paperwork in front of her.

"I'm sorry, Anna," Elsa said glumly. "Maybe next week?"

Anna nodded, disappointed, and left Elsa's study. She knew that her sister had a lot to do. Anna was lucky to have some free time, and she wanted to spend it mountain climbing. The weather was absolutely perfect for it!

Anna put on her cloak and left the castle.

As she walked through the courtyard, the sun's gentle rays slanted down on her. It was beginning to warm up outside. Spring was finally in the air.

On her way into the village, Anna walked past farmers planting wheat in their fields. They pushed their heavy plows, cutting deep furrows in the earth. The smell of damp soil drifted in on the warm breeze. Anna drew a deep breath and smiled. There was nothing quite like a beautiful spring day!

In the distance, Anna saw villagers gathering lingonberries. The fruit was ripe this time of year and ready to be picked. The thought made Anna's stomach rumble. She was looking forward to eating freshly baked lingonberry pies. But pies didn't just happen by themselves. Someone had to pick the lingonberries first. No wonder everyone was so busy!

Anna kept walking. From the fields she made her way down to the docks. Fishermen were hard at work unloading their boats. Sea birds hovered, hoping to catch any fish that slipped from the nets. Soon the townspeople would come to buy fresh seafood to smoke, pickle, and preserve. Anna liked smoked herring, but she couldn't say the same about pickled herring. It was Elsa who liked things pickled.

Anna turned from the docks and headed toward the center of town. On her

way, she spotted Kristoff. He was riding in a large wagon pulled by his reindeer, Sven. The wagon was piled high with ice. Anna waved to him and he came to a stop alongside her.

"Hey, Kristoff," Anna said. "It looks like you have a ton of deliveries to make. Anything I can do to help?"

"Nope," Kristoff replied. "I've got everything under control. You know ice harvesters — *delivery* is our middle name."

Sven nickered in agreement.

"What are you up to today?" Kristoff asked.

"I thought I'd climb Mount Haraldsdottir," Anna answered.

Kristoff's eyes lit up. Haraldsdottir

was one of his favorite peaks. It was a challenging climb, but it was worth it. The view from the summit was spectacular. Kristoff sighed wistfully. "I wish I could go with you," he told her. "But I have too much to do."

"I understand," Anna said. "I was up all night finishing my chores."

"This time of year is always busy," Kristoff said. "It can't be helped."

"Well, good luck with your deliveries," Anna told him.

Kristoff nodded and drove off with Sven to deliver his ice.

Anna walked on through the center of the village. Townspeople hurried by, eager to complete their errands. Even Olaf had plenty to do. The cheerful snowman stood in the middle of the town square. He greeted each villager who passed with a big, warm hug.

"Hi, Anna!" Olaf said brightly as she approached.

"Hello, Olaf," Anna replied. "I was going to invite you to go mountain climbing with me, but it looks like you've got your hands full."

Olaf stared at his tree-branch hands, puzzled. "I don't know, Anna," he said. "They look pretty empty to me."

"I just meant that you look busy," Anna explained.

9

"Oh, I am! You wouldn't believe how many people there are to hug! Hey, you're one of them!" Olaf bounded over to Anna and gave her a big hug. "Where's Elsa?" he asked. "I'll bet she could use a hug, too."

"She's stuck at the castle with a pile of paperwork," Anna answered. "But you're right, Olaf. I'm sure she could use a hug."

"Why don't you give her one?" Olaf said. "I would, but the village needs me here." As if to prove his point, Olaf hugged an unsuspecting farmer on her way across the square. The woman blinked in shock, then smiled gratefully at the snowman, thanking him for the pleasant surprise.

As Anna watched the exchange,

she realized that maybe Olaf was on to something. Arendelle was a busy town, full of busy people, but even busy people needed hugs. Busy people needed time to relax, to sit back and smell the lingonberries.

"That's it!" Anna said suddenly as a brilliant idea took shape.

"What's it?" Olaf asked.

"Don't you worry your busy little head about it," Anna said lightheartedly. "You just keep hugging. I'll handle the rest."

Chapter 2

Anna hurried back to Arendelle Castle. She walked briskly into Elsa's study, only to find her sister nodding off at her desk.

"Elsa!" Anna cried excitedly.

"Huh?" Elsa blurted out as she woke with a start. She blinked rapidly, willing her eyes to focus. A blush of embarrassment crept across her cheeks.

"My point exactly!" Anna exclaimed.

Elsa stared at her blankly.

"The whole town is worn out!" Anna said. "I mean, even the queen is sleeping at her desk!"

"I wasn't sleeping," Elsa murmured sheepishly.

Anna gave her sister a doubtful look.

"Okay, I was taking a tiny nap," Elsa admitted.

Anna walked over to Elsa and placed a hand on her shoulder. "Why take a tiny nap when you can take a great big one?"

"What do you mean?" Elsa asked.

"I mean we need a holiday, Elsa," Anna replied. "I've been all over the village today, and everyone's working really hard.

Arendelle could use a break."

"You're right," Elsa said with a sigh. "I know everyone is exhausted."

"Then declare a special holiday by order of the queen," Anna told her.

Elsa sat back in her chair and thought about it. There was nothing she would've liked more than a day of rest. But there just wasn't time.

"I can't, Anna," Elsa said. "There's barely time enough to finish all the spring projects *without* taking a break. A holiday would put everything way behind schedule."

Anna placed her hands on her hips stubbornly. "Can you give me one example?" she asked.

"Well, take all this, for instance," Elsa replied, waving to the papers on her desk. "I'm supposed to go to Tikaani to offer a trade agreement, but if I leave, there'll be no one to keep all the planting and picking on track."

"Hmm . . . I see what you mean," Anna said.

"A holiday is a wonderful idea, Anna. But maybe after the spring chores are finished," Elsa told her.

"Or," Anna said, thinking out loud, "you could go and *someone else* could make sure all the chores are done."

"But who?" Elsa asked. "Kai is too busy with his butler duties, and Kristoff can't spare a moment with all his ice deliveries.

Olaf is a sweetheart, but I wouldn't leave him in charge. He'd just spend the whole time hugging everyone—"

"Ahem!" Anna interrupted, clearing her throat. "Aren't you forgetting someone?"

Elsa tried to think of people who could run the kingdom while she was away. She counted silently on her fingers. "No, I don't think so," she answered.

"What about *me*?" Anna asked exuberantly.

"You?" Elsa replied, surprised. "But aren't you busy, too?"

"I am," Anna said. "But I can always find time to help."

Elsa stood up behind her desk. She

paced back and forth, considering Anna's idea. "It wouldn't be too much trouble?" she asked.

"Of course not," Anna answered.

"Because that would be absolutely perfect! I could visit Tikaani for a few days, and you could visit the farms and the docks to check in with the villagers," Elsa said delightedly. "Anna, you're brilliant!"

"It is one of my better qualities," Anna replied with a smile.

Elsa gave her sister a hug and hurried off to make arrangements for her trip.

*

Early the next morning, Elsa's traveling trunk was loaded into the royal carriage. The driver waited patiently as the Queen of Arendelle delivered some last-minute instructions to her sister.

"Now, don't forget to inspect the plumbing canals just south of the village. Dagmar noticed a change in water pressure at the village laundry," Elsa explained. "It could be the water pump, but we need to make sure there's nothing blocking the pipes."

"Got it," Anna said with a nod.

"And there's the spice shipment arriving on Tuesday," Elsa told her.

"I remember," Anna replied.

"Plus, the inventory of the food stores should be completed by—"

"Elsa! Will you get in the carriage already?" Anna asked, exasperated. "Trust me, everything will be fine."

Elsa took a deep breath and climbed into the carriage that would take her to the royal ship. She knew Anna was more than capable of running the kingdom, but that didn't stop her from worrying about the villagers. What if they needed her while she was away? Sometimes Elsa felt like a nervous parent leaving her child for the first time.

"Listen, everything will be fine," Anna told her. "I can handle it."

"I know," Elsa responded. Hearing

Anna say it made her relax a little. She sat back in the carriage and tucked herself into her traveling cloak.

"Now, don't *you* forget to say hi to Sivoy and Suqi for me," Anna said. Neither she nor Elsa had seen Tikaani's famous brother-and-sister sled-dog racing champions since the Arendelle Cup competition.

"I'll be sure to tell them," Elsa promised.

"And Kaya, too!"

"And Kaya, too," Elsa confirmed, thinking of the gentle black and white sled dog she'd taken a liking to. She nodded to the driver and he picked up the reins. Within seconds they were under way.

As the carriage made its way across the courtyard, Elsa looked over her shoulder. She saw Anna standing in front of the castle, waving goodbye. Anna smiled confidently at her.

"Have a safe trip, Elsa!" she called.

Chapter 3

Anna took her duties as princess in charge very seriously. The following afternoon, she set out to visit Arendelle's farmers. Her first stop was a large wheat farm on the western edge of the village. The farm had been owned by Engvald Mullener and his family for years. When Anna arrived on horseback, Engvald hurried to greet her.

"Princess Anna! How nice to see you," he said. "What brings you to my farm?"

"I promised Elsa I'd visit to see how the spring planting is going," Anna explained.

"Be my guest," Engvald said, eager to show her around.

The farm stretched as far as the eye could see. Engvald led Anna through field after field of newly turned soil. Some of the soil had already been divided into neat rows ready to be seeded.

"You've done an incredible amount of work here," Anna said, impressed. She knelt down and picked up some of the rich, dark soil. It crumbled easily as she sifted it through her fingers.

"*We've* done an incredible amount of work," Engvald replied, pointing proudly to his wife, Hanne, and their two sons, Per and Lars. Each of them carried a sack full of seeds slung over one shoulder. They walked carefully up and down the rows,

dropping seeds into the earth. During the busy planting season, the whole family worked together on the farm.

When Per and Lars noticed Anna with their father, they dropped their sacks and ran over to see her. Hanne followed, walking quickly behind them.

"Princess Anna!" Lars chirped excitedly. At seven years old, he was still young enough to be thrilled to see the princess. His older brother, Per, was also excited, but he was old enough to hide it. The twelve-year-old met Anna with a quiet smile.

Anna greeted them warmly. She praised both boys for their hard work. Lars told

Anna all about the seeds he'd planted. When he finished, he gave an enormous yawn.

"With all that planting, you must be tired," Anna said. "What time did you get up this morning?"

"We usually get up at dawn and start work right after the family has breakfast," Hanne explained.

"Today we had smoked salmon!" Lars told Anna.

"We sure did," Engvald said. "Then we set to work planting."

"It took all morning," Per spoke up.

"I'll bet," Anna responded, looking out over the acres and acres of land.

27

"Even with all that work, we still have more fields to plow and seed," Engvald said.

"But when do you get to rest?" Anna asked.

"At bedtime!" Lars answered.

"We pretty much work all day, every day, in the spring," Engvald told her.

"And when do you play?" Anna asked the boys.

Lars gave a cheerful shrug. For him, any time spent with his family was a good time.

"We don't mind. The family needs us, and so does the town," Per explained proudly.

Anna pushed up her sleeves and turned to Engvald.

"Is there anything I can do to help?" she said, ready to lend a hand.

"Oh no, Your Highness! I wouldn't hear of it!" he replied politely.

Anna glanced at Per and Lars, her eyes twinkling with mischief. "You won't let me help, eh? Well, suppose I challenge you two to a little seed-off?"

"What's a seed-off?" Lars asked.

"It's when we see who can plant these rows the fastest," Anna replied, pointing to the freshly tilled soil. She picked up a sack full of seeds and crouched low to the ground like a runner at the starting line

of a race. "On your mark . . . Get set . . ."

Per and Lars scrambled to pick up their seed bags.

"Go!" Anna said, and took off running. Quickly, she dropped the seeds into the ground and covered them with mounds of dirt.

The two boys worked in the rows alongside her. Anna was fast, but Per and Lars were faster. They were used to life on the farm.

Engvald and Hanne smiled at the friendly competition. They knew Anna had tricked them into letting her help, but they didn't mind. While Anna and the boys seeded, Engvald and Hanne hitched

up a horse-drawn plow and began to till another field.

"Almost finished!" Lars squealed, nearing the end of his row. Per was right behind him. Anna was in third place but quickly closing in on the brothers. The next few moments were enough to decide the race. Lars came to the end of his row, dropped his seeds into the soil, and patted a handful of dirt on top of them. "I won!" he cried.

Per congratulated Lars with a pat on the back and Anna gave him a hug. "Congratulations!" she said. "You're the winner of the first official Mullener Farm Seed-Off!"

Lars was so excited that he couldn't wait to tell his parents. He raced across the newly planted rows to the field where Engvald and Hanne were hard at work.

"Mom! Dad!" he cried eagerly. Anna and Per hurried after him. But when they reached the field, they were greeted with a strange sight. Hanne and Engvald had shuffled to a stop behind the horse-drawn plow. They'd fallen asleep on their feet!

Lars prepared to wake his parents with a shout, but Anna placed a finger to his lips. "Shhh," she said gently. "I bet your parents are tired."

"But what about the planting?" Per whispered to Anna.

"Sometimes a little rest after a lot of work is a good idea," Anna explained. "It helps you feel refreshed, and then you can work even longer."

"Really?" Lars asked, yawning.

Anna nodded and ruffled the boy's hair. "Never underestimate the power of a nap," she said with a wink.

Chapter 4

Anna spent all afternoon visiting farms. By the time she returned to the castle, she was in good spirits. The spring planting was going according to plan. Arendelle's farmers and their families were working round the clock. Even though they were tired, they were proud to tend the crops they raised for the village. Anna hoped the town's shopkeepers felt the same way during this busy season. Many of them were preserving fruits and fish to sell to families in the coming months.

The next morning, Anna walked to the docks to meet with one of the village shopkeepers, Rona Sorkensson. Rona was a fishmonger. She sold all kinds of fish—fresh, frozen, salted, and smoked. Anna spotted her carrying a large basket along the wharf.

"Let me help with that," Anna called. She hurried over to Rona and took one handle of the basket of fish. Rona thanked her softly. The two women carried the heavy load between them.

"Thanks for meeting me, Princess

Anna," Rona said. "I can't wait to show you my smokehouse."

"I can't wait to see it," Anna replied.

Rona's smokehouse was a small one-room cabin behind her shop. The walls were made of stone, and the roof was covered with weather-beaten wood shingles. It was clear that the little building was old. It had been in Rona's family for a long time. Before Rona even opened the door, Anna caught the strong scent of juniper, one of the woods Rona used to smoke her fish.

"That smells wonderful," Anna said, eager to see inside the cabin.

Rona pushed the door open with her free hand. Together, she and Anna carried the basket of fish into the room.

"Welcome to my smokehouse!" Rona said.

Anna looked around. The place was

empty except for a rectangular work table and a couple of pinewood barrels. The ceiling was very low, and several beams stretched from one side of the cabin to the other. If Anna had been just a bit taller, she might have had to duck!

"I know it doesn't look like much, but this little hut keeps my shop in business," Rona said.

"I think it's pretty neat," Anna told her. "Do you mind showing me how you smoke the fish?"

"I thought you'd never ask," Rona answered. The shopkeeper grabbed an apron hanging from a peg on the wall and handed it to Anna. Anna tied it on and pushed up the sleeves of her dress.

"The first thing we have to do is clean the fish," Rona explained. She opened the large wicker basket that she and Anna had carried in. It was full of fresh salmon. The fish were shiny and smooth to the touch. The tops of their bodies and fins were a deep, dark gray, but their bellies were bright silver.

"They're freckled," Anna said, pointing to several dark flecks of gray that dotted the silver scales.

"I guess they are," Rona replied. "I never thought of it like that." She picked up two fish and carried them to the work table.

First, Rona showed Anna how to clean the fish and cut it into fillets. It was delicate work that had to be done very carefully. Anna was amazed at how quickly Rona could clean a fish. She followed the shopkeeper's directions step by step, but it took her three times as long.

"Don't worry," Rona told Anna. "I've been doing this since I was little."

When the fillets were ready, they took them over to one of the pinewood barrels. Rona popped open the lid and loaded the fish inside. She showed Anna how to pack the fish and cover them with salt.

"The salt absorbs all the water in the fish," Rona explained. "It keeps them from spoiling."

"How long do you keep them in salt?" Anna asked.

41

"Usually a day or so," Rona answered. "It takes that long to draw all the water out. Once that's done, the fish will keep for weeks."

Rona lifted the lid off the second barrel. It was full of fish in a salty liquid that smelled like the sea. "That's called brine," she explained, dipping her fingers in the liquid. "It's all the water that came out of the fish. We packed this barrel yesterday."

Anna helped Rona push the barrel outside. They tipped it over carefully and poured out the brine without spilling the fish. The fillets looked different after a day packed in salt. Originally, they had been bright orange in color. Now they looked darker and were almost transparent.

Curious, Anna reached out to touch the salmon. It felt firmer, too, now that the water had been drawn out.

"Some of my customers like to buy their fish salted just like this," Rona said. She and Anna dragged the barrel back into the smokehouse. "But others prefer it smoked."

"How do we do that?" Anna asked.

"It's an old family secret, but I'm happy to share it with you," Rona said with a wink. She and Anna took the newly salted fish from the barrel. They placed it on the worktable and patted it dry.

"Next we have to hook the fish," Rona explained. She reached into the pocket of her apron and drew out a ball of twine, along with a handful of fishhooks. Rona cut the twine into long strands. Then she taught Anna how to tie the hooks to the ends. Once Anna had finished, Rona slipped the hooks into the fillets.

"Now comes the fun part," said the fishmonger. She picked up a length of twine and dangled the salmon from the end. "It's time to hang the fish from the rafters." Rona looped the twine around one of the low beams in the roof and tied the fillet firmly in place. "Why don't you give it a try?" she said to Anna.

Anna followed Rona's directions, and moments later she'd hung her own fillet right next to the first one.

Rona was impressed. "Good work," she said. "Are you sure you haven't done this before?"

"I'm a fast learner," Anna replied, smiling. Rona handed her another fish. Together, they hung all the salmon from the ceiling.

For Anna, this was an unusual sight. She was used to seeing fish swim in the sea, not float in the air. "It's almost like they're flying," she remarked.

"Stranger things have happened," Rona said. She led Anna from the smokehouse into the courtyard. Anna noticed for the first time that there were large sacks of wood chips next to the cabin. "This is how we give the fish its flavor," Rona said.

"Each sack is filled with a different kind of wood, like juniper or beech."

Rona and Anna gathered wood chips in their apron pockets and carried them into the smokehouse. Inside, Rona arranged them into neat piles on the stone floor. She lit each of the piles with a match and surrounded them with stones from the courtyard.

Soon there were several small fires burning. The smoke from the fires drifted up toward the rafters. It swirled around the hanging fish. A small vent in the roof kept the air flowing freely.

"And there you have it," Rona said proudly. "We let the fish smoke for at least twelve hours."

"That's genius!" Anna exclaimed as the crisp scented smoke tickled her nose. "Do you do all this on your own?"

Rona shook her head. "It's a lot of work for one person," she said. "Thankfully, my cousins Einar and Ida help. It's a family business."

At that moment, there was a knock on the smokehouse door. Rona opened it and her cousins walked in, each carrying a heavy basket of salmon. She introduced them to Anna, who offered to help clean the fish.

"No thank you, Your Highness. We wouldn't dream of interrupting your duties," Einar replied gently, stifling a yawn.

"We know how busy you must be," Ida added. She, too, looked like she could use a nap.

Rona told Anna that she and her cousins could manage just fine. They were used to working long hours during the spring.

"But wouldn't you like a rest?" Anna asked.

Rona thought for a moment. "I guess I wouldn't mind a day to put my feet up," she answered.

"Or race my new sleigh," Einar said wistfully.

"Or sit down to enjoy a nice tasty pie," Ida admitted.

"But there'll be plenty of time for that after spring chores," Rona said.

Anna folded her arms across her chest. She thought about the chores she and Elsa used to do when they were little. One time, their parents, the king and queen, had asked them to help out at the royal stables. The stable master sent them to fill the horse troughs with water. They had to carry heavy buckets back and forth from the stream.

It took a long time, and after a while, Anna and Elsa got tired. They began to walk more slowly. Each trip to and from the stream took longer and longer. When the stable master noticed, he invited them to take a break for lunch. After a good meal and a short rest, Anna and Elsa felt refreshed. They carried the water from the stream with a spring in their steps. They even finished filling the troughs sooner than expected.

"Your Highness?" Rona said, seeing Anna lost in thought.

Anna blinked, turning her attention back to the present. She thanked Rona and her cousins and wished them well with their chores. But as she left the smokehouse, she couldn't stop thinking about the stable master. He'd given her and her sister a chance to take a break from their work, and it had made all the difference to the tired girls.

Chapter 5

The noonday sun hung high overhead when Anna and Olaf hiked out to the lingonberry fields. The little snowman bounced along eagerly beside the princess. He was more than happy to go with Anna on her next visit. This time she was meeting with the villagers picking berries for the spring harvest.

Anna loved berry picking. It was the perfect excuse to walk through the warm, sunny meadows outside town. It also gave her the chance to make friends with the people she met in the fields. Anna couldn't think of one bad thing about picking berries. The hardest part was to keep from eating them all before she brought them home!

"Over there!" Olaf chirped, pointing to a cluster of lingonberry bushes ahead. A small group of villagers was gathered around them. The men and women pulled the round red fruit from the plants and dropped it into their pails.

Anna and Olaf said hello to the berry pickers. "It looks like a beautiful crop this year," Anna remarked with a smile.

"They're perfectly ripe," a villager named Clara replied. She offered Anna a berry from her bucket.

Anna accepted it gratefully. She popped the tiny fruit into her mouth. The tart flavor of the lingonberry spread across her tongue. It was absolutely delicious.

Anna thanked Clara politely. Then she and Olaf set to work. They plucked lingonberries from between the shiny green leaves of the bushes in front of them. Their pails were nearly full, when they heard the sound of a familiar voice.

"Hoo, hoo!"

It was Oaken, the owner of Wandering Oaken's Trading Post and Sauna. The tall, barrel-chested man waved to Anna and Olaf as he approached. He balanced a long wooden pole across his shoulders. At each end of the pole, a large bucket of berries hung from a length of rope.

"Hi, Oaken!" Olaf said brightly. "What's that thing across your shoulders?"

"It's a carrying yoke," Oaken explained. "It helps me carry two bushels of berries at once, *ja?*" The buckets swayed gently as Oaken walked. They were twice as big as the pail in Olaf's twig fingers.

"Two bushels is a lot of berries, Oaken," Anna pointed out. "What'll you use them for?"

"My latest invention," Oaken answered. He lifted the yoke from his shoulders and set the buckets down. "I call it the traveling lingonberry pie!"

"Wow!" Olaf said, amazed. "How does the pie travel? Where does it go? Is it going on vacation?" The snowman frowned trying to imagine it. "I guess even pies need a vacation."

"Good point, Olaf!" Anna chuckled. "What exactly is your invention, Oaken?"

"Simple! I just put the pie on a stick so people can take it with them, *ja?*" Oaken explained.

"You mean, you put an entire pie on a stick?" Olaf asked. His eyes grew wide with wonder.

"Hoo, hoo! Not the whole pie, just a small piece," Oaken said.

"Oh!" Olaf said, catching on. "You can have a traveling pie anywhere!"

"That's right," Oaken said. "You can enjoy my delicious flaky homemade crust packed with sweet lingonberry filling while you do your spring chores. You can enjoy it while planting seeds or picking berries in the fields, or even in the comfort of your very own smokehouse!"

Anna smiled at Oaken's description. It sounded a lot like the way he announced his blowout sales at the trading post. There was no doubt that the traveling pie was a brilliant invention, but something about it bothered Anna.

"Oaken, a traveling pie is a fantastic idea. I just wish people didn't have to take it with them," Anna said.

"But it is so convenient, *ja?*" Oaken asked proudly.

"Oh, it is! I agree. It's just that everyone is so busy! No one has time to sit down and savor your delicious pies anymore."

"Hmm, this is true," Oaken said. "But

it can't be helped. This is a very busy time of year."

Anna narrowed her eyes in thought. This was the second time she'd heard someone say it couldn't be helped. But she was here to help!

"Maybe it *can* be helped," Anna said, considering. "Maybe the biggest help of all would be a whole day to rest."

"And take naps?" Olaf asked enthusiastically. "I love naps!"

"Me too," said Anna. "But not just naps. Time. Time to eat pies sitting down. Time to spend with family and friends."

"Hoo, hoo! That does sound delightful," Oaken said.

"Not just delightful. Necessary!" Anna

exclaimed, eyes shining. "The spring chores are important, but if we work too much, we don't have time to appreciate the things around us. Just look at that beautiful blue sky overhead!"

Olaf, Oaken, and the villagers picking berries looked up at the sky. Fluffy white clouds marched across the horizon on a soft spring breeze.

"Now imagine you could spend as much time as you want staring up at the clouds and daydreaming," Anna said.

Olaf let out a sigh filled with longing. "I think I like daydreaming almost as much as I like summer," the snowman said.

Anna drifted off into a daydream of her own. She imagined the castle courtyard

filled with colorful tents. Each tent was an oasis of relaxation. There were tents for eating, tents for music and games, and tents just to put your feet up. Villagers wandered in and out of each tent with smiling faces. They looked bright and well-rested. They looked relaxed.

"Hoo, hoo! Princess?" Oaken said, snapping Anna out of her fantasy.

"Oaken, I just had the most wonderful daydream," Anna told him through a grin. "And since I'm princess in charge, I'm about to make that dream a reality."

Chapter 6

While Anna was having visions of a well-rested village, Elsa had just finished meeting with the leaders of Tikaani. The village elders were happy to make a trade deal with her. They agreed to supply Arendelle with much-needed wool in exchange for delicious lingonberries.

Elsa thanked the elders graciously and took her leave. She stepped outside their igloo into a charming snow-covered landscape. Tikaani was located on an island that was farther north than Arendelle. That meant the weather was a lot colder. Even though it was spring here, the ground was still blanketed with snow.

Elsa realized that because of the snow, the spring chores in Tikaani were different from the chores in Arendelle. Instead of planting wheat or picking berries, the villagers here were busy ice fishing and gathering wool and spinning it into thread. The thought of chores made Elsa wonder how Anna was getting along. She hoped that by now her sister had visited the farmers and the berry pickers and the villagers who smoked the fish. There were so many things to keep track of during this busy season. Elsa really wanted to make sure that all the spring projects back home were on schedule.

Suddenly, Elsa heard the sound of barking dogs. She looked up to see her friends Sivoy and Suqi approaching by dog sled. The brother-and-sister pair were known for their well-trained team of dogs. Their four-legged friends had helped them win many a sled-dog race.

Suqi waved excitedly to Elsa as the sled came to a stop. She handed the reins to her brother and hopped down to give Elsa a hug.

"It's so good to see you!" Suqi said cheerfully.

"You too!" Elsa replied. The last time she'd seen Suqi and Sivoy had been at the Arendelle Cup race. They'd ended up co-champions with Elsa and Anna.

Sivoy tied up the sled and then gave Elsa a friendly hug. "We thought you might like to meet the newest members of our racing team," he said.

"Newest?" Elsa asked.

"That's right," Suqi answered. "Kaya had puppies a few weeks ago."

"Six of them," Sivoy said proudly.

Kaya usually ran at the head of the sled-dog team, but today she was home with her pups.

"That's amazing!" Elsa replied. "I'd love to meet them!"

Moments later, the three friends were racing across the snowy plains. Elsa rode in the back of the sled, grateful for the opportunity to catch up with Sivoy and Suqi. "Anna and I love getting your letters," Elsa told them. "I'm only sorry I haven't been able to write more often."

"That's okay," Suqi said. "We know being queen must keep you busy."

"We're just glad you're here now," Sivoy told Elsa. He smiled at her and flicked the reins, urging the dogs faster.

"What have you two been up to?" Elsa asked the siblings.

"We're training for our next race," Suqi explained.

"And helping Kaya with her pups," said Sivoy. "Sometimes they're a bit of a handful."

"It sounds like they got that from their mother," Elsa said. She remembered that Kaya had an independent streak. Once, she'd sneaked out of the royal kennels in Arendelle to hunt for her masters inside the castle. Suqi and Sivoy smiled ruefully. They continued to chat pleasantly with Elsa for the rest of the ride.

A short while later, Sivoy pulled back on the reins. The team of dogs slowed down and came to a stop in front of an igloo.

"Welcome to our home," Suqi said. She and Sivoy led Elsa inside. In the middle of the room, on a pile of furs, were Kaya and her puppies. As soon as she saw Elsa, Kaya padded over to her, tail wagging with excitement. Elsa knelt down to scratch Kaya's ears. The sled dog licked her face affectionately.

Kaya's puppies bounded after her and surrounded Elsa in a sea of furry bodies. They were all black and white like their mother, with bright blue eyes. They sniffed Elsa curiously on unsteady legs. Some of them nudged her gently with their noses.

"They're adorable," Elsa said. "How old are they?"

"About eight weeks," Sivoy answered. "They've just opened their eyes."

"They're already starting to develop personalities," Suqi said.

After a few minutes with the puppies, Elsa noticed their personalities, too. The first pup greeted her right away, while the second seemed to hang back. The third puppy wandered past Elsa toward the door, ready to explore outside. Kaya gently picked him up with her mouth and carried him back to his brothers and sisters. The fourth puppy gnawed the hem of Elsa's dress, while the fifth tried to climb into her lap. The last pup unleashed a tiny bark, seemingly pleased by the sound.

"How long before they start learning to pull a sled?" Elsa asked.

"It'll be a few more weeks yet," Sivoy said. "They're still just learning to be dogs."

Elsa petted the puppies softly as they romped around her. Soon they began to grow sleepy. They tottered back to the pile of furs on the floor and wriggled together in a heap. Within seconds their eyes slipped closed and they drifted off to sleep. Kaya curled up next to her pups, keeping a watchful eye on them.

Elsa was surprised at how quickly the puppies had fallen asleep. "It looks like they wore themselves out," she said.

Sivoy nodded. "Puppies are learning all the time. They're hard workers that way. Sleep helps them to develop and grow," he said.

"Not to mention it restores their energy," Suqi explained. "As soon as they wake up, they'll be running and bouncing all over the place."

"I guess there's something to be said for taking a break," Elsa said thoughtfully.

"It's true," Suqi said. "Our dogs work hard pulling sleds, but they definitely know how to relax."

Sivoy smiled proudly as he looked at the pile of sleeping puppies. "We can learn a lot from them," he said.

∗

After her visit with Sivoy and Suqi, Elsa was eager to get news from Arendelle. She wrote a quick letter to Anna asking about the spring chores. The letter was full of questions. Did the farmers need help with the planting? Had the fishermen caught enough fish to salt and smoke? Was the lingonberry harvest going according to plan?

Elsa knew that Anna could handle any challenge, but that didn't stop her from worrying. Most of her worry had to do with being so far away. She felt guilty for not being there to help if the villagers needed her.

Elsa was relieved when the messenger from Arendelle arrived. He was ready to carry her letter back to the kingdom. She placed the letter in his hands and gave him careful instructions. "Please get this to Arendelle as fast as you can," she said.

"And deliver it directly to Princess Anna."

The messenger nodded. He gave Elsa a polite bow. "I'll try my best, Your Majesty," he said. "But with the holiday, things might take a little longer than usual."

"Holiday?" Elsa asked, surprised. "What holiday?"

"Princess Anna has declared a Day of Relaxation," the messenger explained.

Elsa was astonished. She thought that maybe she'd heard him wrong. There wasn't time for a holiday during one of the busiest weeks of the year!

Chapter 7

The following morning, Anna stood outside of the gates of Arendelle Castle. The huge wooden doors had remained open ever since Elsa became queen, but today they were closed for Anna's big surprise. Most of the villagers had gathered in front of the castle walls to find out what she had in store.

"Hello, everyone!" Anna said brightly. "As you all know, I've named today an official day of rest!"

The crowd cheered heartily. They were looking forward to a break from all their hard work.

"Today your only goal should be to unwind and spend time with the people you love! I've set up a few activities to help you do just that," Anna told the villagers, pointing to the gates behind her. "So without further ado, welcome to Arendelle's one and only Oasis of Relaxation!"

Anna signaled to the palace guards to open the gates. The heavy doors swung inward, revealing the castle courtyard,

which had been utterly transformed. Multicolored tents and booths stretched out across the cobblestone plaza in neat, orderly rows. Each tent and booth served up its own relaxing specialty.

Anna ushered the villagers into the courtyard. She was extremely pleased by the wide smiles on their faces. Many of them had looked so worried lately. It was nice to see them calm and peaceful instead as they strolled back and forth. Soon they were visiting the tents and lining up at the booths to buy tasty treats.

Anna made her way through the crowd and stopped outside the Napping Tent. She had come up with the idea after visiting Engvald and his family. The huge red-and-white-striped pavilion had a pointed canopy with a pennant on top that flapped gently in the breeze. The pennant was decorated with fancy letters that read ZZZZZZZZ. It was clear that this tent had one purpose and one purpose only: it was the perfect place to sleep.

Anna stepped inside the pavilion and was greeted by the sound of silence. The entire space was filled with comfortable quilts, plush pillows, and napping villagers. Kai the butler kept a watchful eye on the sleepers. It was his job to make sure the tent stayed quiet. He moved carefully between the townspeople, offered extra blankets and sleep masks, and gently nudged anyone who snored too loudly.

Satisfied that the villagers had everything they needed for a peaceful sleep, Anna turned to leave. On her way out she spotted Engvald, Hanne, Per, and Lars. They were all snuggled up in blankets next to each other, fast asleep. Lars even clutched a stuffed reindeer in his arms. Anna smiled. She couldn't wait for them to wake up feeling refreshed and full of energy.

Anna walked out of the Napping Tent and back into the Oasis of Relaxation. She saw Olaf just a few feet away with Kristoff and Sven. The mountain man and his reindeer had volunteered to play relaxing music for the crowd. Kristoff strummed his lute and sang soothing songs while Sven kept time with the beat of his hooves. Anna joined her friends and listened to Kristoff sing one of Sven's favorite lullabies.

There's no deer like a reindeer,
'Cause reindeer are the best.
They're loyal friends
Until the end
Who work without much rest.
So if you love your reindeer,
You'll give him lots of care
With carrots, hay,
And time for play,
'Cause even reindeer

Need a day

To just kick up their hooves

And say:

Reindeer are the best.

Anna and Olaf clapped enthusiastically when Kristoff finished his song, but no one seemed to appreciate the lullaby more than Sven. The reindeer showed his

gratitude by licking Kristoff's face with a big, noisy *SLURP!* "Aw, thanks, buddy," Kristoff said, before wiping his face with his sleeve.

"Great job, Kristoff!" Anna said. "Very soothing, especially for the reindeer."

"That's my goal—to soothe reindeer and people alike," Kristoff replied. "But I have to admit, all this soothing is making me hungry."

"Let's visit Oaken's pie booth," Anna suggested. She guided Olaf, Kristoff, and Sven across the courtyard. They arrived just in time to see Oaken hand a lingonberry pie to another satisfied customer.

"Hi, Oaken," Olaf said. "How're the traveling pie sales?"

"No traveling pies today," Oaken answered.

"How come?" Olaf asked.

"Today is a day of rest, *ja?*" Oaken replied. "There is no need to enjoy a pie on the go. Everyone has time to sit down and savor a whole pie, bite by delicious bite." Oaken winked playfully at Anna, who nodded in agreement. "This reminds me," he continued, checking his pocket watch. "It's time for the pie-eating contest."

Oaken clapped his hands to get everyone's attention. "Hoo, hoo!" he called. "Who would like to join a competition to eat delicious lingonberry pie?"

Within moments Oaken had more than

enough contestants. He seated them all at a long table that had been set up next to his booth. In front of each villager, he placed a lingonberry pie. When everyone had received a fork and knife, Oaken looked at his watch again. "Ready . . . set . . . GO!" he shouted.

Olaf was ready to keep track of all the fast-paced action. But instead, the contestants moved slowly. They cut into their pies, lifted their forks to their mouths, and chewed at a snail's pace. Olaf blinked in surprise.

Kristoff also noticed the peculiar pace. "This is the strangest pie-eating contest I've ever seen," he said.

"That's because the rules are different, *ja?*" Oaken told him.

Anna watched the contestants curiously. The slower they moved, the more they seemed to appreciate every bite. "I think I understand," Anna said, catching on. "It's not about how fast you can eat a pie, it's about how *slow*!"

"Correct," Oaken replied. "The slowest contestant wins."

"That doesn't sound so hard," Kristoff said, patting his stomach.

"It's tougher than you think. My pies are so tasty everyone is in a hurry to gobble them up," Oaken explained. "But only those who take their time will truly experience the deliciousness."

"Oaken, you're a genius!" Anna exclaimed.

"And proprietor of Wandering Oaken's Trading Post and Sauna, *ja?* Don't forget that part," he said.

"So when does the contest end?" Olaf asked.

"When the last person has taken the last bite," Oaken replied.

"This could last all night," Anna said, watching the contestants.

"Hoo, hoo! This is true," Oaken pointed out, but he wasn't worried in the least. "In the meantime, could I offer you some pie, Princess Anna?"

"Absolutely!" Anna said. Oaken served her a fresh slice of lingonberry pie and she gobbled it up in an instant. Fortunately, she wasn't participating in Oaken's contest, or she would have lost immediately! Kristoff had a slice of pie, too, and it made him even hungrier. He lifted his head and caught the delectable smell of smoked salmon on the breeze. Almost without realizing it, Kristoff and Sven drifted toward the scent. Anna and Olaf said goodbye to Oaken and followed their friends. The delicious smell led them to a stand where Rona the fishmonger was selling her wares.

Rona greeted Kristoff, Sven, Anna, and Olaf with a smile. "Look, Your Highness," she said to Anna. "These are the fish you helped to smoke." She held up a tray of thinly sliced smoked salmon ready to eat.

Anna was eager to taste the fish she'd helped to make, but Kristoff beat her to it. He scooped up a piece of salmon and shoveled it into his mouth.

"This is delicious!" he mumbled between mouthfuls.

Anna gave Kristoff a look that said *Where are your manners?*

"Sorry," Kristoff said sheepishly. "I was really hungry."

Rona didn't seem to mind at all. She offered Kristoff another piece of fish and then served Anna her salmon on a slice of thick bread. As Anna tasted the fish,

she thought fondly of Rona's smokehouse. She remembered the pale orange fillets hanging in the cabin scented with juniper smoke. Now the salmon had a salty, smoky flavor. Anna decided it was the yummiest fish she'd ever had.

"I'll buy a pound," she said to Rona. Anna couldn't wait to bring the fish home for dinner.

"Buy? I couldn't let you pay. It's on me," Rona explained. She wrapped the fish neatly in heavy paper and secured the bundle with a string. "After all, I'd never charge an honorary fishmonger."

Anna was flattered.

"All hail Anna of Arendelle, Honorary

Fishmonger and Bringer of the Day of Rest!" Kristoff joked.

"Don't forget princess in charge," Anna added.

"And princess in charge!" Olaf echoed cheerfully.

Anna grinned from ear to ear. She liked the sound of that.

Chapter 8

Early the next morning, as soon as the royal ship docked in Arendelle, Elsa hurried down the gangway. She was hoping to find out just what the messenger had meant by "Day of Relaxation." Relaxing was something Elsa associated with summer, when the warm temperatures and long days filled with sunlight encouraged everyone to unwind. Spring in Arendelle was the hectic season, filled with plans, projects, and to-do lists. Relaxing now seemed like a highly unusual idea.

Elsa borrowed a horse at the docks and rode quickly toward the castle. She was surprised to see so many townspeople out and about this early in the morning. She thought she'd find the streets of the village empty because of the holiday. Instead, it looked just like any other busy morning in town.

"Hello there, Your Majesty! Welcome back!" cried a voice.

Elsa turned her head to see Engvald the

farmer driving a wagon full of farming equipment. He had just made the long journey from the supply depot. But he didn't look at all tired. In fact, he appeared sprightly and well rested. Elsa slowed her horse and pulled alongside him to say hello.

"Good morning, Engvald. How are

things at the farm?" Elsa asked.

"They're going quite well, Your Majesty. In fact, Princess Anna's visit really turned everything around," Engvald told her. "Do you know that she ordered a Day of Relaxation?"

"I heard," Elsa said hesitantly. "But it looks pretty busy here to me."

"The holiday was yesterday," Engvald explained. "It was wonderful! Princess Anna created an Oasis of Relaxation. There was a Napping Tent and everything!"

Napping Tent? Elsa thought. It seemed like a great idea, but she wasn't sure how taking a nap was going to help anyone with their chores. "I'm glad you got the chance to rest yesterday," Elsa told him.

"But if you were in the Napping Tent, who was planting the wheat?"

"No one," Engvald answered happily. "Everyone took the day off."

To Elsa's surprise, Engvald wasn't the least bit worried about the planting schedule. Instead, he seemed full of energy and good cheer. She watched, amazed, as Engvald said farewell and drove off toward his farm.

Elsa nudged her horse gently and continued to ride toward the castle. On her way through the town square, she saw Rona the fishmonger carrying a large basket of fresh fish. Elsa stopped and offered to help.

"That's okay, Your Majesty, I can make

it on my own," Rona said politely, shifting the basket to her hip. "After the day of rest, I feel as good as new."

"That's great, Rona," Elsa replied. "But do we have enough smoked fish to store for the season?"

"Well, the inventory is low after all the fish we sold yesterday," Rona explained. "The Day of Relaxation really increased sales."

"I see," Elsa said. "But what if we run out of fish?"

"Not to worry," Rona replied. "We'll make more."

With that, the fishmonger waved goodbye, shifted her basket, and turned in to the lane that led to her smokehouse.

Even though Rona had said not to worry, Elsa felt slightly uneasy. As queen, she wanted to be sure that there was enough wheat and fish to keep everyone well-fed, especially later in the year, when the village prepared for winter. Not to mention that Arendelle traded crops with other countries, like Tikaani. Elsa had just promised them lingonberries in exchange for wool. If the kingdom hadn't picked enough lingonberries, she might have to cancel the trade.

That thought made Elsa change her course. She guided her horse to the lingonberry fields to check on the status of

the picking. As she rode into the meadows, she was greeted by Oaken. He carried two large buckets of berries that hung from a yoke across his shoulders.

"Hoo, hoo! Welcome home, Queen Elsa!" Oaken called out.

Elsa was relieved to see him carrying so many lingonberries at once. It gave her hope that, at least when it came to picking fruit, the village was still on schedule. But then she noticed that Oaken was the only one in the fields.

"Hello, Oaken," Elsa said. "Where is everyone?"

"They will be along later, *ja?*" he answered pleasantly. Like Engvald, Oaken was cheerful and well rested. He didn't seem worried about falling behind schedule.

Elsa, on the other hand, grew more nervous. Now more than ever she wanted to talk to Anna. She'd asked Anna to make sure to keep all the projects on track, and the empty fields had her worried.

Elsa said goodbye to Oaken and rode the rest of the way to the castle as fast as she could.

When she arrived, she raced inside looking for Anna. Anna wasn't in her bedroom, or the kitchens or the library. Instead, Elsa found her in the study. She was sitting behind Elsa's desk checking inventory records. Elsa couldn't help noticing that Anna looked absolutely worry-free and every inch the princess in charge.

Chapter 9

"Elsa! You're back sooner than expected," Anna said brightly. She hopped to her feet and gave her sister a great big hug.

Elsa was happy to see Anna, but by now she was really concerned. "Anna, I came back to help as soon as I could. Is everything on schedule?" she asked.

"Of course," Anna said with a mysterious smile.

Elsa recognized the look on her sister's face. It was one part mischief and two parts determination.

"Even with the holiday?" asked Elsa.

"Especially *because of* the holiday," Anna answered.

"What do you mean?" Elsa said.

"I mean that everything is going according to plan," Anna replied cheerfully. "Allow me to show you."

*

Anna's first stop was Engvald's farm. She and Elsa walked through the newly planted fields. When they reached the barn, Engvald, Hanne, Per, and Lars emerged carrying sacks full of seeds. They hurried to make Anna and Elsa feel welcome, especially Lars. He greeted the queen and the princess with a sweeping bow.

Anna curtseyed in return.

"You won't believe how much we got done!" Lars told her. "Papa says we'll have the afternoon off to play!"

"It's true," Engvald said. "That day of rest really helped. We can work twice as fast on a good night's sleep."

"We feel so refreshed," Hanne added. "The boys are practically bouncing with energy."

Both boys took the opportunity to lead Anna and Elsa to the large field south of the barn. When Anna had visited a couple of days ago, it hadn't been planted. Now it was nearly finished.

"You did all this in one morning?" Anna asked, impressed.

Per nodded. "We all worked together," he said.

Elsa was astonished. She'd been so concerned with staying on schedule, she hadn't considered that stopping to rest might actually make the work go faster. "That's incredible!" she exclaimed.

Anna gave her sister a knowing smile.

*

A short while later, Anna and Elsa visited Rona's smokehouse. They met the fishmonger in the courtyard gathering juniper chips in her apron.

"Good to see you again, Your Majesty, Your Highness," Rona said.

"How's the fish smoking coming along?" Anna asked. "I can't wait to bring home more delicious smoked salmon for dinner."

"Does this answer your question?" Rona asked playfully. She opened the door to the smokehouse and led Anna and Elsa inside. The ceiling beams were completely strung with fish fillets swirling in scented smoke. Through the foggy air, Anna could see a flurry of activity. Rona's cousins Einar and Ida were working steadily along with a few other villagers.

"With all the money we made from yesterday's sales, I was able to hire some new helpers," Rona explained. "We've got twice as many people to help with the salting, curing, and pickling."

"What a fantastic idea!" Elsa remarked.

"I'll say," Anna responded in agreement. "With the extra help, you'll have more inventory in no time."

"I can't thank you both enough for the holiday," Rona said.

"It was Anna's idea," Elsa replied, giving credit to her sister.

"Sure, but it was you who left her in charge," Rona pointed out. "The two of you make an excellent team."

Anna and Elsa exchanged a look.

"I couldn't agree more," said Elsa.

✳

The final stop on Anna's tour of the kingdom was the lingonberry fields. This was the second time Elsa had been there today, but now the meadows looked very different. They were swarming with berry pickers! And that wasn't all. Elsa noticed that each of the villagers picking berries wore a carrying yoke just like Oaken's.

Oaken himself was loading buckets of lingonberries into a horse-drawn wagon. He acknowledged Anna and Elsa with a friendly wave. "Hoo, hoo!" he said. "What brings Your Majesty to the fields again?"

"I was wondering about the lingon-berries," Elsa spoke up. "Do you think we have enough berries to trade?"

"Enough to trade, enough to eat, and enough for my pies!" Oaken answered enthusiastically. "After the holiday, everyone is picking so much faster, *ja?*"

Elsa looked out across the fields. The townspeople seemed to be picking at double the speed. She also realized that with their new yokes, people could carry twice as many berries as before. That meant the villagers had to empty their buckets less often. The result was that they could spend more time picking!

"The yokes seem to make everything easier," Elsa said.

"Oh yes, that was Princess Anna's idea," Oaken replied. "She saw my yoke and asked if I could show the villagers how to make their own."

"Is that where everyone was this morning?" Elsa asked, remembering the empty fields.

"Yes," Oaken answered, nodding.

Elsa turned to Anna, who was gazing out over the meadows with a broad smile. She could tell that Anna was proud to have helped the villagers.

"I'm sorry I doubted you, Anna," Elsa said. "I was just so worried about getting everything done on time."

"I know," Anna said. "But sometimes when things get really busy, it helps to take a tiny break. Like that time we carried buckets of water to the stables."

"Oh!" Elsa said. "I remember. We got so tired, but after lunch we finished in no time."

"That's why I thought a holiday could help," Anna told her. "I was inspired by

every bucket we carried—and every break we took—together."

Elsa gave her sister an apologetic hug. She knew Anna was right—sometimes you had to slow down in order to speed up. She only wished she had agreed to the holiday the first time Anna had asked. "I don't know why I didn't see it sooner," Elsa said.

"Well, you know me. I always see things a little differently," Anna joked.

"And thank goodness for that!" Elsa replied. "It's exactly the kind of inspired thinking I'd expect from the princess in charge."

Chapter 10

Early the next morning, Elsa had an inspired idea of her own. Standing just outside Engvald's farm, the queen raised her arms and swirled her fingers through the air. Anna watched as frost gathered around Elsa's fingertips. It always amazed her to see her sister's powers in action. They were truly magical.

Elsa shaped the frost into a sparkling wave of ice and created a long, winding ramp from the farm to the village supply depot. When Engvald and his family woke, they were greeted by a startling sight. They rushed outside to speak to Elsa and Anna.

"What's all this?" Engvald asked.

"It's an ice ramp," Elsa answered. "I saw you driving home from the depot yesterday. It's a long ride, so I thought I'd give you something to make it shorter."

"Thank you so much, Your Majesty," Engvald said, touched.

Hanne, too, was moved by Elsa's gift. She gave Elsa a grateful hug, then watched her sons scramble up onto the ramp. Per and Lars shouted gleefully as they sped down the icy slide.

*

By afternoon, Arendelle was full of Elsa's ice slides. They wound their way through the village, circling houses and snaking through the streets. The townspeople were more than thrilled with this slippery new way of traveling, especially Rona the fishmonger. Her ramp went directly from the docks to her smokehouse. Now she could slide fish home from the wharf instead of carrying them.

"Your ice ramps are a hit," Anna told Elsa. "They save so much time!"

They were standing at the end of Elsa's longest ramp yet. This one was shaped more like a chute. It ran all the way from Oaken's Trading Post to his new pie stand in the middle of the village. Oaken planned to use the chute to send his lingonberry pies into town, and he'd asked Anna and Elsa to help with his first shipment. The sisters had agreed to wait at the end of the chute to catch the pies.

"Did Oaken send those pies already?" Elsa asked.

"I think so," Anna said.

They'd been waiting for nearly five minutes when they heard the sound of pie pans skittering on ice.

"Here they come!" Anna said. She moved into position at the bottom of the chute. Moments later, the first pie came flying. Anna caught it quickly, but she wasn't prepared for the second and third pies. They flew out of the chute just seconds later. One splattered on Anna's dress, while the other crashed to the ground.

"I didn't know pies could move so fast!" Anna exclaimed.

Elsa hurried over to help her sister. The pies continued to fly out of the chute at top speed. Elsa managed to catch one, but they were coming much too quickly. She and Anna chased and dove after the pies. Unfortunately, they couldn't possibly catch them all. Elsa was left with no choice. She created a wall of ice to block the pies and keep them from tumbling to the ground.

Finally, the chute was empty. Anna and

Elsa flopped to the ground, exhausted by their pie-chasing efforts.

"What do we tell Oaken?" Elsa said at last. She looked from the pie stains on her dress to the smashed chunks of pie on the ground.

Anna smiled. "We'll think of something," she said. "But first, I think I need another Day of Relaxation."

Elsa laughed. She couldn't have agreed more.